A Note from the Author

Many years ago I was in a plane that flew into a storm. I've never been so scared in my life. Luckily, both the pilot and co-pilot were good at their jobs. But what if something had happened to them? I was thinking about this when I wrote my ghost story *Gremlin*. I hope the ending takes you by surprise ...

For Jake, Polly and Suzie, who will be readers one day ... and maybe pilots, too.

Contents

Chapter 1
A Problem in the Air

I was going to die.

We were all going to die – every one of us.

That's what was in my mind when the Chief Steward came stumbling past the other passengers. He bent down beside my seat. "Are you Glenn Jago?" he said softly.

"That's me."

"How are you doing, Glenn?"

"Fine," I told him. "If it wasn't for all this."

I waved a hand around me. The jumbo jet was tossing like a ship at sea. In one set of cabin windows there was nothing but sky. In the other, nothing but mountains.

Mountains and sky ... sky and mountains. It was as if two giants were tipping the plane to and fro. One wanted to keep us flying. The other wanted to smash us on the rocks below.

"What's the pilot up to?" I asked.

"You tell me."

The Chief Steward lifted a finger to his lips. He didn't want to wake the other passengers. I saw how white his face was. "We've got a problem, Glenn," he said. "We need your help."

"*My* help?"

"You're our only hope."

I gritted my teeth. That was the last thing I wanted to hear.

"OK," I said. "What's the problem?"

"We've got a Gremlin."

"Sorry?"

"A Gremlin," said the Chief Steward.

OK, I'd heard him the first time. I knew just what he was telling me. Also, why he'd come to me in the first place. It was a word I'd known since I was a kid.

Gremlin.

Now I was sure we were going to die.

Chapter 2
Flashback

I first heard the word 20 years ago.

I was 10 years old at the time. "Gremlin?"

I said. "What's a Gremlin, Dad?"

"Ah ..." said Dad.

He took his shiny old brown pipe out of his mouth. That's when I knew I'd asked an important question. Dad always kept his pipe handy – even when he was flying a plane. He liked the feel of it, he said. Even when it wasn't lit, it helped him think. Here at home, he smoked all the time. Lots of people did when I was a boy.

Dad tapped the pipe on his knee. "Gremlins are hard to explain," he said. "Do you believe in ghosts, Glenn?"

"Sometimes."

"And do you believe in luck?"

"Good luck or bad luck, Dad?"

"Both."

"Yes, I do."

"Then maybe you believe in Gremlins.
A Gremlin is a kind of ghost who travels by
plane. Sometimes it brings good luck and
sometimes bad. Which it is depends on the
Gremlin."

"Does every plane have a Gremlin, Dad?"

"Some pilots think so. Others reckon there's no such thing. They say Gremlins are just a story. But watch them closely when they say this. Often they've got their fingers crossed!"

"What do you believe, Dad?"

Dad puffed at his pipe for a while. Its sweet, chestnut smell drifted around his study. I watched his face as I waited. It was a fine, strong face. Would I look like him one day? And would I be half as good a pilot?

At last he spoke. "I believe in proper training, Glenn. I believe in skill. I believe in checking every detail before the plane takes off. After that, I believe in keeping your mind on the job all the time you're in the air. Flying isn't about good luck or bad luck – it's about doing the best you can for all the people on board."

"So you don't believe in Gremlins?"

"No, I don't."

Dad shook his head. Then I spotted his left hand – the hand that wasn't holding the pipe.

Why had he crossed his fingers?

Chapter 3
Dad's Death

Dad was a great pilot. He'd always been extra-special. He could fly any kind of plane there was – from a glider to a jump-jet. He was a test pilot. He was a stunt-pilot at air shows. He was a pilot who wrote best-selling books about flying. In fact, he was a hero to just about every other

_____

pilot in the world. Most of them knew by heart his FIVE RULES FOR BEING A FLYER:

1. Proper training.

2. Skill.

3. Checking every detail before take-off.

4. Keeping your mind on the job all the time you're in the air.

5. Doing the best you can for everyone on board.

To him, these rules were vital. Then, one day when he was flying across the Andes – the biggest mountains in South America – the rules didn't matter a jot. His plane simply vanished along with his crew, his passengers and himself. No radio message was ever sent. No wreck was ever found. His famous unlit pipe, with its sweet chestnut smell, had gone forever.

No-one knew what had gone wrong. The crash was a total mystery. Maybe that's why the stories began ... about an extra passenger who hadn't bought a ticket.

Yes, a Gremlin.

I just refused to listen. Dad would have hated an excuse like that. Good luck or bad ... a pilot must cope with both. Only a wimp needs to put the blame on a ghost.

Anyway, that was 20 years ago.

Chapter 4
Back to the Present

Right now, 20 years later, I was glaring at the Chief Steward. "Look," I snapped. "My name is Glenn Jago not Scott Jago. I'm not a famous pilot like my father. In fact, I'm not a pilot at all any more. I gave up training half-way through Flying School."

"After you heard your father had crashed?"

"About then, yes."

The Chief Steward nodded. "I can understand that," he said. "But I bet you've never stopped asking questions, Glenn. Why else are you on this flight across the Andes?"

"Because ..."

"Yes?"

"Because I need ..."

"Because you need to find out what really happened? Glenn, maybe it's happening again right now. Just think for a moment. What would your dad be doing if he were here in your place?"

"I keep telling you," I said. "Dad was a one-off. I'm a different person from him."

"How different, Glenn?"

I couldn't tell him. The truth is, I wasn't sure. But already I could see that the swaying of the plane was waking up other passengers. I undid my seatbelt. "OK," I said. "Let's play it your way. What do you want me to do?"

"Come to the cock-pit," said the Chief Steward.

The cock-pit?

My heart sank at once. The cock-pit is the nerve centre of any plane. If that's where this so-called 'Gremlin' was hanging out then we were in real trouble.

Chapter 5
The Cock-pit

Getting to the cock-pit wasn't easy. The rock-and-roll of the jumbo jet was getting worse with every second. "What's wrong, Steward?" someone shouted as we staggered past.

"A bit of a bumpy ride, that's all."

"Anything to worry about?"

"Not yet, sir," the Chief Steward said. "We'll let you know when to panic."

This made the man smile. Other passengers smiled, too. I did my best to smile back but that was just for show. This plane had a Captain, didn't it? With a co-pilot to back him up? Why weren't *they* dealing with the bumpy ride?

I soon found out.

The Chief Steward prodded me through a thick curtain. He pulled this tight shut behind him. We were in the galley where the food and drink is kept. Beyond this was the cock-pit. On the door was a notice in big, black letters:

CREW MEMBERS ONLY

"After you," he said.

Me?

Was I a crew member now?

I pushed open the door of the cock-pit. Inside were two more stewards. One was bending over the Captain who lay slumped on the cock-pit floor. The other was gripping the co-pilot's hands to stop them shaking.

"What's going on?" I gasped.

"The Captain's had a heart attack, Glenn. It's bad, I think. I'm not sure we can save him."

"What about the co-pilot?"

"A panic attack," said the Chief Steward, dryly. "I'm not sure we can save him, either."

"Isn't there a doctor or a nurse on board?"

"First thing we thought of. We checked the passenger list over and over again. No luck, I'm afraid. There are no other pilots, either. You're the best we could come up with."

His face was grey with worry. In a crisis as bad as ours, I could see why people had invented Gremlins. For the moment, the jumbo jet was flying itself on auto-pilot. But that couldn't last much longer. Already I felt I was the wrong person for the job. Scott Jago was the pilot we really needed.

Glenn Jago was who we'd got.

Chapter 6
Taking Over

When was the last time I'd sat in a pilot's seat? Was it 10 years ago at Flying School?

At least that long. And even then it was never a seat like this one. All round me were dials and switches and levers. I seemed to have three planes to fly, not one. Where should I begin?

Computers blipped.

Warning lights blinked.

Display screens buzzed and flickered.

Every inch of the panel in front of me seemed to say: ME FIRST! ME FIRST! ME FIRST! As I peered through the cock-pit windscreen, I saw nothing but mountains.

Soon there would be just one mountain – with what was left of the jumbo jet and its passengers scattered over its slopes.

Stay cool, Glenn. Stay *cool* ...

Suddenly, I found my voice. It sounded so harsh. Could it really be mine?

"Clear the cock-pit," I rapped out. "Get those pilots into the galley. Don't let the passengers see them. Keep away from me for a while. I need to sort this out on my own."

"On your own?" said the Chief Steward.

"Trust me."

At first they didn't want to. Then I heard the shuffle of feet and a few muttered words. The door of the cock-pit clunked shut. Now, I must trust myself.

Already I'd scanned the panel for the information I needed. I switched off the auto-pilot and put on the radio headset. Gently I pulled back the yoke to lift the plane's nose. "Mayday! Mayday!" I called.

"This is Air America Flight Six Zero Nine. We have an emergency. Mayday! Mayday! Mayday!"

The radio crackled in my ears. "This is Control at Cali to Air America Flight Six Zero Nine. We're receiving you loud and clear. Confirm your position, please."

"Six Zero Nine at 24,000 feet ... estimated time of arrival 20 minutes from now. Do you read me?" I replied.

"You're on-screen now, Flight Six Zero Nine," they said. "Give details of your emergency, please."

"Both pilots are too ill to fly."

"What?"

"Repeat – the Captain and his co-pilot aren't flying this plane. It's a passenger who's making this call."

"You're a passenger, you say?"

"That's right."

"Shall we talk you down?"

"Sounds good to me," I said. "But nice and easy please, Control Tower. Nothing too clever or fancy. I've never flown anything bigger than a six-seater. And that was 10 years ago."

"10 years ago?"

"That's right."

The radio went silent for a moment. When it came back the voice from someone else – someone older and more friendly. "No problem, Six Zero Nine. Let's handle this one step at a time. When it's over I'll buy you a drink in the Cali bar. What's your name by the way?"

"Jago," I said. "Glenn Jago."

"Jago? You're not – "

"His son," I said. "And I'm nothing like my father. So have back-up ready and waiting, OK?"

"Done and dusted, Glenn."

They'd have back-up ready and waiting
all right. Every ambulance, every fire truck
and every medic at Cali would be standing
by now. Once they'd cleared a runway and
fixed our flight path, they would put the
whole airport on red alert. After all, they'd
got a half-trained pilot on their hands.
Half-trained 10 years ago, what's more.
Things didn't look too good for Air America
Flight Six Zero Nine. But it was going to
get worse.

The radio packed up.

It gave a splutter and died – just like that. And that's how it stayed in spite of all my jiggling. Forget Cali Control talking us down. Now we had no contact at all. Maybe the Gremlin – the one I didn't believe in – was having his last laugh.

Chapter 7
In the Zone

So I kept my mind on the job.

Most of the time, I used the yoke and the throttle to hold our heading, our height and our air-speed more or less in balance. And somehow, I got away with it.

Heading perfect.

Height perfect.

Air-speed perfect.

By the time I could see the air-field at
Cali I was almost enjoying myself. Soon I
was ready to lower our wheels. I reached
for the tyre-shaped lever under the throttle.
Without even checking the flight manual,
I knew this worked our landing gear.

I was on a roll.

My eyes, my hands and my brain had raised their game well above what was normal. Sometimes a top footballer – or a top tennis player – feels like this. They call it 'in the zone'. And that's where I was ... in the zone as a pilot.

What was going on?

I didn't dare ask. Something seemed to be telling me what to do, that's all – some skill, or memory, or instinct I didn't know I had. Thank goodness I'd pushed the Chief Steward's talk about Gremlins to the back of my mind. I felt so good about being a pilot again, I could have landed that plane on a postcard, never mind on a run-way.

What a fool I was.

Our wheels were only feet from the ground when the fire truck shot across our path. Was it late for the emergency line-up? Or had it just taken a wrong turn? Who can say? Suddenly, it was smack in front of us – impossible to miss.

No wonder I freaked out.

I shut my eyes tight.

I screamed in utter panic.

Already I could see the full horror in my head – a sudden fire-ball, black and crimson, as Air America Flight Six Zero Nine exploded on impact.

Chapter 8
Gremlin

But it didn't happen. In real life, there wasn't any fire-ball that grey winter morning. Air America Flight Six Zero Nine, with all its passengers and crew, escaped without a scratch.

What saved us?

They told me I did.

There's even film footage to prove it. It shows a jumbo jet lifting itself over a fire truck in a kind of giant bunny-hop. "A brilliant bit of flying!" the news media agreed. "Not a single person was injured – even the plane's Captain got to hospital just in time. Flight Six Zero Nine was on the brink of disaster. Instead, it was the most amazing air-escape ever! Thank goodness there was a hero on board ..."

OK, so they were right about the hero.

But the hero wasn't me.

Here's the true story – the one I've been trying to tell ever since. It was my hands on the yoke and the throttle, I admit. Like the rest of me, they were stuck in panic mode. Yet, somehow, they shifted just at the right moment. It was as if someone was working me like a puppet. We went up and over that fire truck with only a foot or two to spare.

After that, the plane made a perfect landing. You can read all about it in the report that came later. The inspectors said that Air America Flight Six Zero Nine had been plain unlucky. The Captain's heart attack, his co-pilot's panic, the broken radio, the mistake by the driver of the fire truck had been one damn thing after another. These things could have happened on any flight.

No-one wanted to know about the Gremlin.

Not that I blame them. Gremlins are tricky at the best of times. Some of them are devils, it's true. And some of them are angels.

I didn't spot this myself till right at the very end. That's when the Chief Steward came crashing through the door behind me. "Glenn, you were fantastic!" he shouted. "Quite fantastic! I've never seen such flying in all my life!"

Then he stopped and sniffed the air. "Hey," he said. "Has someone been smoking in here?"

"Smoking?" I blinked.

I took a sniff myself.

And at last I understood. How could I have missed it? The sweet chestnut smell of a shiny old brown pipe seemed to fill every nook and cranny of the cock-pit. The scent was so strong it took me back more than 20 years. It had helped Dad think, I suppose, while he did his best for Air America Flight Six Zero Nine.

Barrington Stoke would like to thank all its readers for commenting on the manuscript before publication and in particular:

Dalton Cracknell

Will Crisp

P. A. Douglas

Josh Ham

Stella Isaacs

Sam Lawrey

Richard Long

Ryan Marshall

Alex McCann

Luke Pinkham

Tom Ramwell

Joe Sewell

Luke Tompkins

Stuart Watson

Jacqui Wilson

Cath Wolverson

Zakery Wright

Become a Consultant!

Would you like to give us feedback on our titles before they are published? Contact us at the address below – we'd love to hear from you!

Email: info@barringtonstoke.co.uk
Website: www.barringtonstoke.co.uk

Great reads – no problem!

Barrington Stoke books are:

Great stories – from thrillers to comedy to horror, and all by the best writers around!

No hassle – fast reads with no boring bits, and a story that doesn't let go of you till the last page.

Short – the perfect size for a fast, fun read.

We use our own font and paper to make it easier to read our books. And we ask teenagers like you, who want a no-hassle read, to check every book before it's published.

That way, we know for sure that every Barrington Stoke book is a great read for everyone.

Check out www.barringtonstoke.co.uk for more info about Barrington Stoke and our books!

More books by the same author!

Thing

Black button eyes.

Zig-zag mouth.

Stiff body.

Thing.

Once it was Robbie's best friend.

Now it's become his enemy …

You can order *Thing* directly from our website at
www.barringtonstoke.co.uk

More books by the same author!

Fight

My mate could take you.

Matt's mate is a big, tough guy.

So that must make Matt hard too …

Or does it?

You can order *Fight* directly from our website at
www.barringtonstoke.co.uk

More books by the same author!

Blade

STAY AWAY FROM TOXON

That's what they tell Rich.

They tell him about the Blade too, and what it can do to you.

But Rich is in the wrong place at the wrong time.